Churchy and the Light on Christmas Eve

written by Greg Spangenberg

illustrated by Sarah Lodwick

Churchy and the Light on Christmas Eve
is written by Greg Spangenberg
illustrated by Sarah Lodwick
Copyright 2005, Greg Spangenberg

Published and Printed by:
    Lifevest Publishing
    4901 E. Dry Creek Rd., #170
    Centennial, CO 80122
    www.lifevestpublishing.com

Printed in the United States of America

I.S.B.N. 1-59879-017-X

To Lora,
my wonderful daughter who has
always loved the church mouse stories.
Now my adviser and editor, without you
the book would have never been a reality!

To all my children and grandkids.
Be bold in your witness. Remember,
the only Bible that some people
will read is the way
believers live
their lives.

Churchy and the Light on Christmas Eve

From The Adventures Of Churchy Church Mouse And His Cousin Tootsie

Volume I

Foreword

Dear Reader,

Churchy Church Mouse was born within my imagination over 30 years ago. After telling his story to my children and most recently my grandchildren, I've been prompted by them to share his adventures with you. Churchy is much like you and me. He so desires to grow in faith and share it with others, yet faces struggles and insecurities at various times. My hope is that you and your little ones who listen will grow along with Churchy as he matures in his walk with the Lord and becomes a gentle but bold witness to unbelievers, such as his lively cousin Tootsie.

Come along with me as I present to you Volume I of the Churchy Church Mouse Christmas stories. Watch for more tales to come as our mouse friend becomes more confident in his walk with the Savior.

In His hand,

Greg

(John 10:28)

It was a gloomy Christmas Eve for Churchy Church Mouse. Instead of celebrating, he found himself sitting on top of a communion cup beside a hole in the wall he now called home. Churchy sighed as he looked out over his new church building.

The people had not decorated for Christmas and he didn't know why. Last year the church building he lived in sparkled with decorations, including a freshly cut tree with colorful lights and a bright star on top.

The tree had always been one of his favorite things at Christmas. He liked to climb on it and play with the ornaments. It was also a great place to hide during the church service. He could get a great view of all the people, especially when he climbed to the top and hid behind the star.

But not this year.

Feeling sort of low and lonely, he decided to go downtown to see if perhaps he could find his cousin Tootsie. Tootsie had said that she was spending a lot of time downtown these days. All she talked about lately were the colorful lights and decorations up and down Main Street.

Tootsie liked to move around from place to place, so Churchy wasn't exactly sure where he might find her. But one thing was for sure, she wouldn't go far from downtown.

Churchy wondered if maybe she had moved over by one of the big government buildings. As he thought more about it, he remembered that she had mentioned something about a huge decorated tree outside of City Hall.

Yeah, he thought, that Tootsie is a downtown girl alright. She sure likes to see all the people going every which direction. According to her, it's even more exciting these days with everybody buying presents and having parties.

Even if he didn't find her, he pondered, surely it would cheer him up to see all the people and the bright lights.

So off he went, down the busy street . . . ***Whoom! Whoom!*** . . . went the cars, trucks and busses . . . ***Whoom! Whoom!***

Soon Churchy spotted a bus at a bus stop. Quickly he ran to catch it. The bus started to move, but the door was still open, so he jumped on. He found what appeared to be a safe spot under one of the seats as the bus moved along. He sure hoped this bus was headed downtown.

The little mouse suddenly realized that in his haste to get downtown, he hadn't bothered to pray about his venture. So, he bowed his head right there under the bus seat and said, "Lord, I heard the Sunday School teacher say last Sunday that we can pray to You about anything. Will You help me find my cousin Tootsie? She doesn't believe in You like I do, but I hope You will still help me find her. I'm a little bit scared to go downtown by myself, but with You watching over me, I'm sure I'll be alright. In Jesus name I ask, Amen."

Churchy couldn't see outside as the bus traveled along, but the people were o-o-ohing and a-a-ahing about all the lights, painted store windows and street decorations.

All of a sudden he heard a young boy yell, "Look at the big Christmas tree at City Hall!" Oh WOW! He had to see that. So, when the bus stopped and the door opened, out he bounced.

Cautiously, the little mouse crossed the busy street and sure enough, WOW! There it was -- a tree that lit up the building steps with hundreds . . . no, thousands of colorful lights. Oh, and yes, a star lit the very top with its twinkling light reflecting off the side of the big building.

The fascinated mouse tried to get closer for an even better look, but the people were pushing and shoving, also trying to get closer. Churchy decided to stay back a safe distance. After all, he didn't want to find himself under a shoe!

Nervously turning toward the street, he watched as cars and busses zoomed by and people rushed every which way.

Churchy decided he wasn't as excited about all the lights and glitter as he had thought he would be. As a matter of fact, he found himself getting a little shaky thinking about the possibility of getting squashed on these busy streets. Then he remembered his prayer. He had asked God for protection.

Looking for a place to relax a bit, Churchy found himself being drawn to a curious little light off by itself in the city park. He looked for an opening through all the shoes on the sidewalk and vehicles on the street and . . . *Zoom!* . . . off he ran toward the light.

"It's a Nativity!" Churchy exclaimed with delight. A little barn-like structure with figures of Mary and Joseph watching over the Baby Jesus stood all by itself in the vacant park. The mysterious light was a star shining down on Jesus' face.

"Where are all the people?" Churchy whispered. But even as he spoke, it occurred to him: *All the people are over at the shops buying presents and looking at the big Christmas tree. It is so peaceful here at the Nativity.* He felt so good inside.

Soon this quiet, peaceful place made the little mouse feel sleepy. He glanced over to the corner of the barn and noticed an inviting pile of straw. He thought that it might be a good idea to lie down for a few moments to just rest and enjoy the Nativity.

Churchy climbed up on the pile of straw, snuggled in a bit . . . suddenly the straw began to move!

With one frightened leap, he was off the pile of straw. He watched as the straw pile came apart. What do you know? Out popped Tootsie!

"What are you doing here, Tootsie?" he barely could squeak.

"I live here," Tootsie declared.

"You what?" asked Churchy.

"Yeah!" said Tootsie, "Every year some people put up this barn and these figures here in the park. It's warm and quiet, so I move in. I get to see all the decorations, the big Christmas tree and all the people running around. Hardly anyone comes over here."

"But Tootsie," exclaimed Churchy, excited for the opportunity to share, "this is what Christmas is all about: The Baby Jesus! He is King of Kings and Lord of Lords. He is the Light of the World and He was born on Christmas Day!"

"Oh Churchy, settle down. No King would be born in a barn."

"Jesus was," said Churchy. "Mary and Joseph had traveled to Bethlehem and there was no place to stay. Mary was going to have a baby, the Baby Jesus."

"Well, it's a good story," said Tootsie, "but if Jesus was a real king, why do they put Him over here in the park by Himself and not under the big Christmas tree?"

Churchy had to think on that question for a moment. He said, "I guess because where Jesus was born it was a quiet place, too. The only people who came to see Him were shepherds. An angel told them where to find the Baby."

"You've got quite a story there, Churchy," said Tootsie, "but I've heard enough about angels, shepherds and quiet places. I want to par-r-r-rty!"

"Party," said the little church mouse. "I've never been to a party."

"Well, we can fix that," said Tootsie. "I heard some people talking yesterday about a big Christmas party over on 10th Street. Let's run over and see if we can find it."

"O-okay . . . I guess," replied the hesitant church mouse.

So they took off for 10th Street and sure enough, they found a huge decorated house with cars and people everywhere . . . the par-r-rty place.

"Churchy, let's go in!" said Tootsie.

"O-o-okay, I g-guess" said the very reluctant friend.

They quickly slipped through the door and immediately hugged the wall. There were a lot of feet! People were eating, drinking, laughing and even singing some Christmas songs.

The house decorations were beautiful, but the floor looked the most inviting to the two hungry mice. Crumbs of all kinds had fallen just out of their reach: Gingerbread cookie crumbs, sugar cookie crumbs, chocolate and spice cake crumbs, Christmas pie crumbs.

"Look! Do you see it?" whispered the excited Tootsie. A delicious piece of peppermint had caught her eye.

"Yes, I see it," said Churchy, "but it's out there in the middle of all those feet. You can't go out there. It's too DANGEROUS!"

Tootsie couldn't stand it. To her, the big piece of candy was worth the risk. So without another word, she ran into the dangerous maze of feet. She dodged cowboy boots, loafers, flats and high heels. Safely she reached the candy. But, on the way back . . . Boom!

A big boot stepped right on her tail. Biting down on the candy kept her from squealing. Even though it really hurt, she didn't want to scream. The people might panic and she'd get squashed for sure.

She bit down extra hard on the candy and waited until the person moved. Then back to the wall she scurried.

"Was it worth it?" asked Churchy.

"Oh, my tail is so sore," moaned Tootsie, "but look at this big piece of candy!"

"I see it," said Churchy, "but I wouldn't have tried that."

Churchy, feeling sorry for Tootsie, said, "Let's go see if we can find a bandage to put on that tail."

"O-okay, I g-guess," said the whimpering Tootsie. They slipped into the next room, looked around and found themselves next to a huge bed.

"Tootsie, look how big this bed is," said Churchy. "The people have piled a mountain of coats on it."

"Yeah, yeah," said Tootsie, "b-ut w-hat a-bout my t-ail?"

"Listen!" said Churchy, "what was that?"

"W-hat was w-hat?" moaned Tootsie. "D-id y-ou f-orget a-bout my t-ail?"

"Listen!" said Churchy again. That time Tootsie heard it, too.

"It sounds like a whimper from a baby!" shouted Churchy.

"Where did it come from?" asked Tootsie.

"On the bed," said Churchy. "Let's climb up and look!"

They climbed up on the bed, but all they could see was an enormous pile of coats. Then once again, they heard the little muffled cry.

"Tootsie, it's a baby and it's under the coats!" said Churchy. "Somebody must have put the baby on the bed to sleep and forgotten about it. The people have piled their coats on the bed not knowing the baby is here. Help me pull them off!"

They pulled and tugged . . . but it wasn't working.

"Tootsie!" yelled Churchy. "The coats are too heavy! We can't pull them off and I don't hear the baby anymore! I'm not sure it can breathe! What can we do?"

The fast thinking Tootsie said, "Maybe if we run out into the other room, climb up on the big food table and squeal, the people will want to leave. They will come and get their coats."

"It's worth a try!" said the scared church mouse.

Out they ran to the main room, climbed up the back side of the food table and shrieked . . . *"E-e-e-e-e-k!"*

People started screaming and pushing each other. Then all of a sudden, a woman screamed, *"The baby!"* and ran to the bedroom as fast as she could.

Everyone in the room froze with fright and it became very quiet. The woman screamed again, *"Oh no!"* Everyone stood still, waiting. Suddenly, a loud cry came from the baby.

Tootsie and Churchy looked at each other and smiled. They knew the baby had been rescued.

Both Churchy and Tootsie were feeling pretty good about what they had done.

Then to their surprise . . . *WHACK!* Someone smacked them both with a newspaper and their small bodies went flying off the table.

When they hit the floor, they ran out of the house as fast as their little legs could go.

The two little mice didn't say anything to each other as they walked back toward the park. It was late and the streets were almost deserted. Even though Churchy was walking beside Tootsie, he felt a sense of loneliness. Then he realized this was a good time for prayer.

Churchy started walking a little slower as he prayed. Tootsie walked on ahead. He thanked God for helping him find Tootsie and for watching out for them at the party place. He also thanked God for the opportunity to help save the baby on the bed. Yet, at the end of his prayer, he still had a heavy heart.

After walking a little further, he realized it was hard to enjoy this Christmas Eve, thinking that Tootsie still didn't have a clue of what Christmas is really about.

Churchy stopped, looked up and said, "God, what can I do to help Tootsie see the Light?"

Churchy suddenly realized that Tootsie was nowhere in sight, so he took off running to catch up with her.

When he got to the park, Tootsie had already reached the Nativity. She was just standing there staring up at Baby Jesus in the manger.

"Tootsie, are you okay?" asked Churchy.

Tootsie didn't say anything at first, but finally she managed to say, "That is what is happening to Baby Jesus, isn't it?"

"What?" asked Churchy.

Tootsie turned to her friend and said, "People are having parties, decorating trees, buying presents, going here and there and they have just about smothered the Baby of Christmas."

There was a long pause as the little church mouse hung his head in thought. "Yeah, I think you are right," whispered Churchy, as a tear ran down his cheek.

Tootsie looked back at the manger, then back at Churchy. "I'm going to sleep with Baby Jesus tonight," she whispered.

"Oh wow," whispered Churchy, "what a great idea."

They climbed up in the manger and snuggled up to the feet of Jesus.

Suddenly Churchy said, "Tootsie?"

"Yeah?"

"Listen." Off in the distance they could hear some people singing, "Silent Night, Holy Night, all is calm, all is bright . . ."

To Order Copies of

Churchy and the Light
on
Christmas Eve

by **Greg Spangenberg**

$14.99
$2.00 Shipping/handling

I.S.B.N. 1-59879-017-X

Order Online at:
www.authorstobelievein.com

By Phone Toll Free at:
1-877-843-1007

By Mail:
Lifevest Publishing
Churchy and the Light on Christmas Eve
4901 E. Dry Creek Road #170
Centennial, Colorado 80122